E   Stickland, Paul

621

Tools

DATE DUE   *1-13-99*

DATE DUE

MR 17	AP 27	MY 22 '77	
JY 27			
AP 01	AP 30 '12		
AP 29	JY 30 '12		
	NO 09 '12		
16	AG 21 '13		
14	NO 07		
AG 31			
DE 20	AP 20		

DEMCO 128-5046

WORKING

TOOLS

**For a free color catalog describing Gareth Stevens'
list of high-quality books and multimedia programs,
call 1-800-542-2595 (USA) or 1-800-461-9120 (Canada).
Gareth Stevens Publishing's Fax: (414) 225-0377.
See our catalog, too, on the World Wide Web:
http://gsinc.com**

Library of Congress Cataloging-in-Publication Data

Stickland, Paul.
    Tools / Paul Stickland.
      p. cm. — (Working)
    Includes index.
    Summary: Presents a group of tools and a situation in which
they might be used such as a spade to plant a tree, scissors to
cut the fabric for a dress, and a wrench to tighten a nut on a
bicycle wheel.
    ISBN 0-8368-2159-9 (lib. bdg.)
    1. Tools—Juvenile literature. [1. Tools.] I. Title. II. Series:
Stickland, Paul. Working.
TJ1195.S75   1998
621.9—dc21   98-13648

This North American edition first published in 1998 by
Gareth Stevens Publishing
1555 North RiverCenter Drive, Suite 201
Milwaukee, Wisconsin 53212 USA

© 1991 by Paul Stickland. Designed by Herman Lelie.
Produced by Mathew Price Ltd.,
The Old Glove Factory, Bristol Road,
Sherborne, Dorset DT9 4HP, England.
Additional end matter © 1998 by Gareth Stevens, Inc.

Gareth Stevens series editor: Dorothy L. Gibbs
Editorial assistant: Diane Laska

Printed in Hong Kong

1 2 3 4 5 6 7 8 9 02 01 00 99 98

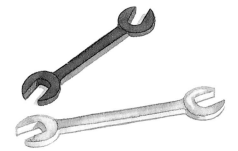

WORKING
TOOLS

Paul Stickland

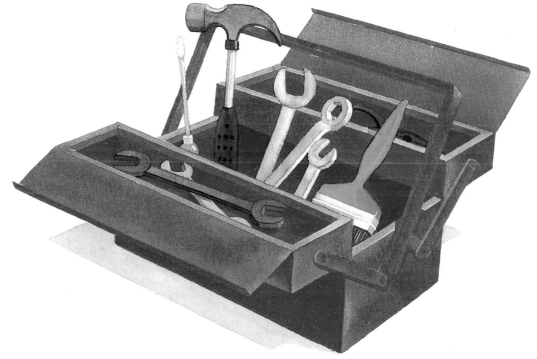

Gareth Stevens Publishing
MILWAUKEE

1-13-99

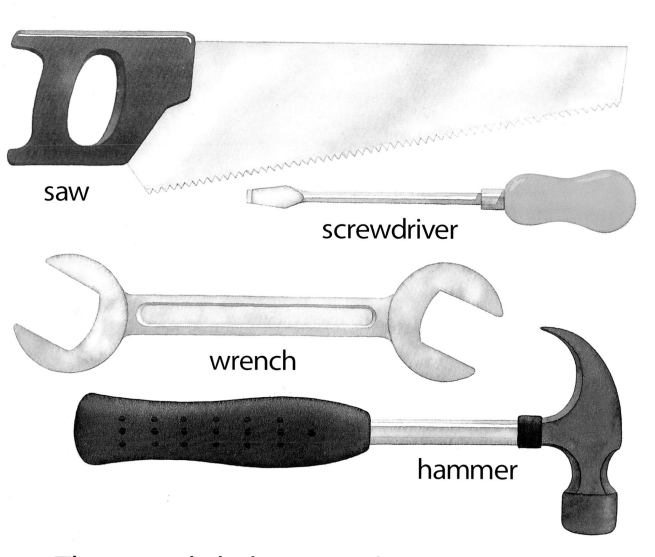

saw

screwdriver

wrench

hammer

These tools help us work.
How are they used? Let's find out!

ax

paintbrush

scissors

tape measure

spade

5

This carpenter is using a hammer to pound nails into wooden beams.

A saw has hundreds of very sharp teeth
that can cut through wood.

A bicycle wheel will come off if the nut is loose. Use a wrench to tighten it.

Scissors are very sharp. You can use
them to cut cloth to make a dress.

You can use a paintbrush to spread
paint evenly over a wall.

One more chop with the ax and this
dead tree will crash to the ground.

Is this cabinet too big for the doorway?
Use a tape measure to find out.

A spade is used for digging. Young trees will be planted in these holes.

You can use a screwdriver to put some
new hooks onto a door.

If the screws get loose, you can use the screwdriver again to tighten them.

GLOSSARY

beam — a long, heavy piece of wood or metal that is used in buildings to hold up floors, walls, and roofs.

cabinet — a piece of furniture that usually has doors and shelves or drawers and looks like a cupboard.

carpenter — a person who uses wood to build things or who fixes things made of wood.

nut — a small piece of metal that has a hole through it with grooves cut on the inside to fit tightly around a screw.

spread (v) — to evenly cover a surface with a thin layer of something.

wrench — a tool used to hold, twist, or turn things, such as pipes, nuts, and bolts.

INDEX